MY HEAD IS RED
and Other Riddle Rhymes

MY HEAD IS RED

and Other Riddle Rhymes

by Myra Cohn Livingston

illustrated by Tere LoPrete

Holiday House / New York

Library of Congress Cataloging-in-Publication Data

Livingston, Myra Cohn.
  My head is red and other riddle poems / Myra Cohn Livingston;
illustrated by Tere LoPrete—1st ed.
      p.   cm.
  Summary: Readers may guess what each of twenty-seven brief poems
describes.
  ISBN 0-8234-0806-X
  1. Riddles, Juvenile. [I. Riddles. 2. American poetry.]
I. Title.
PN6371.5.L5   1990
818'.5402—dc20   89-24528   CIP   AC

Blow us up
and watch our skin
growing bigger.
Twist us in!

Tie us!
See us floating there
high above you
in the air.

BALLOONS

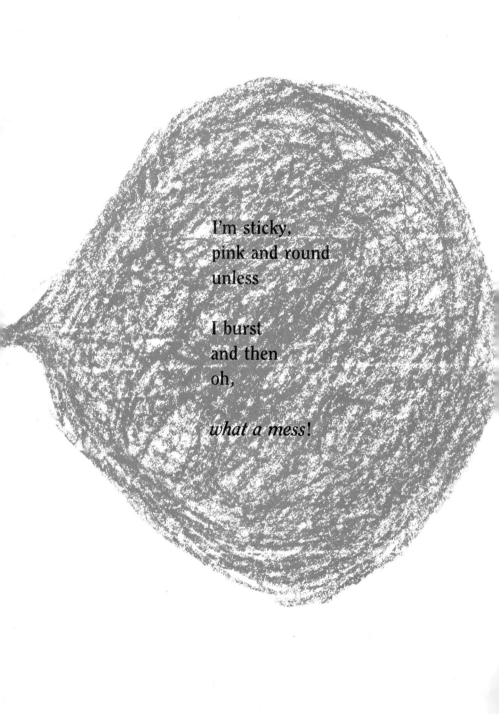

I'm sticky,
pink and round
unless

I burst
and then
oh,

what a mess!

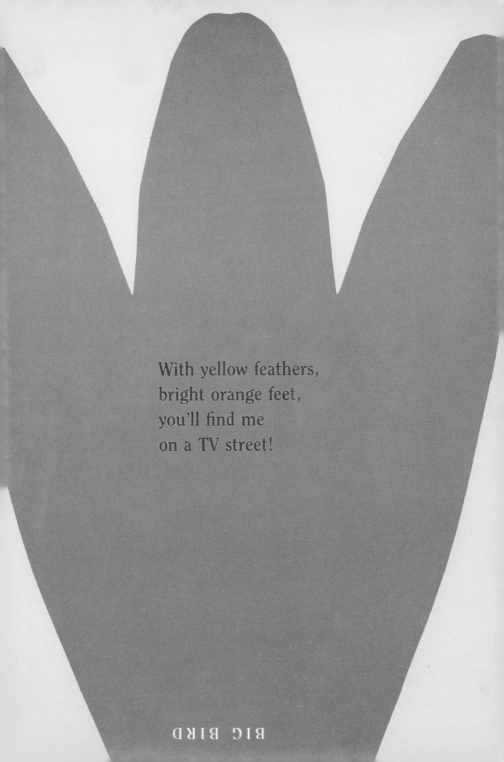

With yellow feathers,
bright orange feet,
you'll find me
on a TV street!

BIG BIRD

Once they roamed
        the earth alone.

Now they're fossil.
Now they're bone.
Now they're skeletons;

You see them
in the halls of great
museums.

DINOSAURS

Four legs,
a head,
a foot,
two sides

and cuddly warm
and soft
insides!

A BED

No neck,
One back,
No head,
Four feet,
Sometimes
Two arms
and always
A seat.

A CHAIR

Closed, I am a mystery.
Open, I will always be
a friend with whom you think and see.

Closed, there's nothing I can say.
Open, we can dream and stray
to other worlds, far and away.

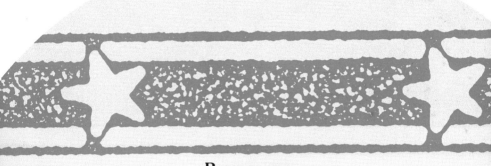

Bounce me
and I'll
go somewhere.
Throw me
and I'll sail
through air.
Hit me
and I'll
fly astray.
Kick me
and I'll
roll away.

A BALL

Give me water!
Don't forget,
I only work
When I am wet!

A SPONGE

With silver spears
I hold my prey
Until you bite it
All away!

A FORK

My head is red.
My back is white.
You'll find me near the
candlelight.

But once I make
a shining flame
I never, ever look the
same.

A MATCH

Blue legs,
Two legs
    hang in the closet.

Blue legs,
Two legs
    run out to play.

Blue legs,
Two legs
    fit on your legs.

Will *you* wear blue legs today?

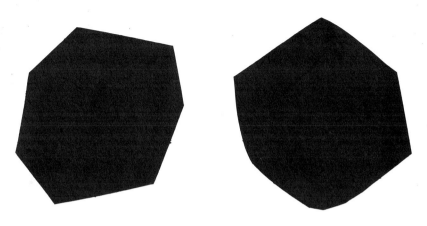

He stands
where it is bitter cold.

Now who do you suppose
could live outside in snow
and wear
a carrot
for a nose?

A SNOW MAN

Below your nose,
above your chin,
we talk
and whistle
and gobble food in!

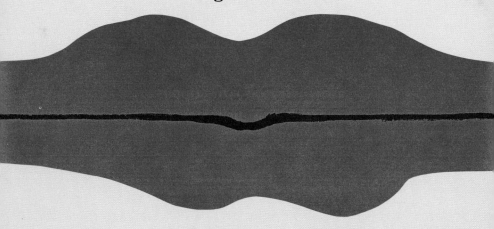

LIPS

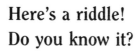

Here's a riddle!
Do you know it?

When it drips
I want to
blow it.

When it's wet
I want to
mop it.

When it runs
I want to
stop it.

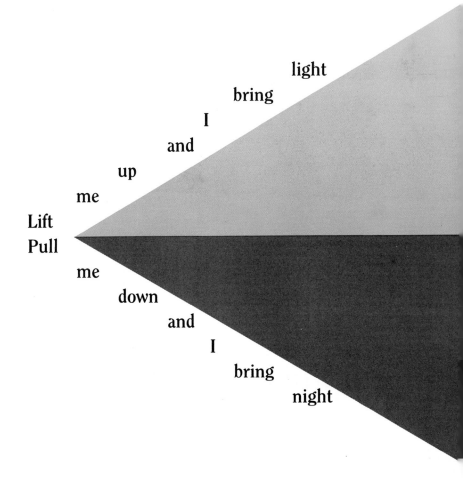

light

bring

I

and

up

me

Lift
Pull

me

down

and

I

bring

night

A WINDOW SHADE

You never see me,
  yet you know
  whenever I come out to blow.

You never see me,
  yet you stay
  to watch me at my wild play.

You never see me,
  yet you hear
  my mournful music in your ear.

THE WIND

In bright yellow coats
all in a row,
We sleep through the summer
with no place to go.

In August we wake up,
guzzle our fuel,
And stop at the corner
to take you to school.

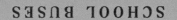

SCHOOL BUSES

In the morning
    I arise
bringing yellow
    to the skies.

At day's end
    I go to bed
covered up
    in scarves of red.

Gray and blue,
  crested with foam,
We are the sailors'
  salty home.

Blue and gray,
  crashing, we roar,
Bringing the sailors
  back to shore.

One click
and
everything
you
do
will reappear
and
look
at
you!

A CAMERA

When I sputter and rumble and pop,
When my lava pours out and won't stop,
When my insides all churn
And my throat starts to burn,
Do you blame me for blowing my top?

A VOLCANO

Dressed in
purple,
black
and
gray,
I come to
chase
away
the
day.

Squeeze me and hug me
and hold me all night.
You'll leave me at last
when the morning shines bright.

What am I?

I polka dot the window,
I shine the blackened street.
I make a mirror of the walk
  And steam the summer heat.

I run along the gutter.
I give the grass a drink.
I splash in lakes and rivers
And into earth I sink.

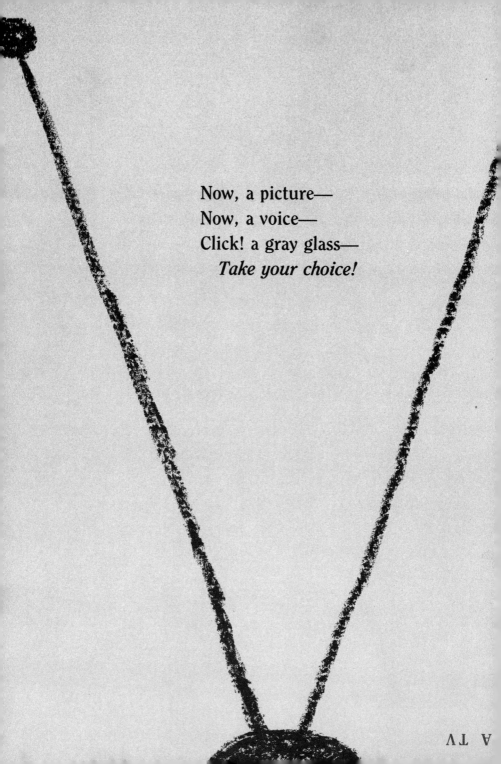

Now, a picture—
Now, a voice—
Click! a gray glass—
Take your choice!

A TV

Stretch my ribs out wide and high
And I will try to keep you dry!

AN UMBRELLA